The Spiritual Nature of Atomic Structure

I0587642

By Patsy Stanley

Copyright © 2018. Use of any part of this book without permission from the authors representatives or agents is prohibited by law. All Rights reserved. No part of this book may be reproduced, transferred, modified, or used in part in any way and in any form without the express written consent of the author.

ISBN 978-1-7326193-5-7

LCCN 2018908828

In the Beginning, was the Word...

There is an ancient force, older than time, made of equal parts of dark and light, that lives within each of us...

Everything is on its way to somewhere....

Auriel or Uriel–is the Regent of the Element of Earth. Sandalphon or Malkuth, The living Sphere of Earth, and Auriel, have an interlinked relationship, each being a regent of a dense aspect of force.

Sandalphon – rules structure of life forms within this planet. Our evolution of consciousness, and of form upon this Earth - the people ruled over by "souls of fire", the symbolic name for the consciousness of the Atom....

"The key to understanding our universe lies in understanding the structure and detail of a single atom."

-Dion Fortune-

We live and have our being in a vast sea of energy created by the two great, opposing Cosmic Poles.

"To understand atomic structure is to understand how God and the Universe work..."

-Dion Fortune-

"To further an understanding of the three energies and how they were formed, we must delve into the Duality, which are the Color and Elemental Mysteries, Mythologies, and all Philosophies."

-Patsy Stanley-

Something Sacred is always at stake

We are constantly bathed in more than one energy from the universe; Universal, Galactic, Galactic Super cluster, Solar system, Sun and Planetary Cosmic energies. And, there are many divisions of Cosmic labor. We take part in Cosmic tasks that have to do with each of these systems.

The universe and everything in it is made of atoms. Every atom we are made of was created somewhere out there in the universe. Where we come from is the same place the Elements came from. We are made of Elements. Atoms are the building blocks of the Universe, the Earth, and all of the living and non living matter around us. The smallest possible amount of Matter that still retains its identity as a chemical element is the atom. Everything is made up of atoms. Atoms are indestructible. Chemical reactions may result in their rearrangement, but not their creation or destruction. Atoms group themselves into cells, molecules, and into larger and larger forms, (including Hue-mans). All of them are made of atoms.

All parts of our being, our physical, emotional, mental and soul bodies residing on the different planes of energy vibrations, are all made up of atoms moving at different speeds.
   o   There are three parts in every Atom:

- The electron
- The proton
- The neutron

   o   The Electron carries a negative charge of energy.
   o   The Proton carries a positive charge of energy.
   o   Neutrons have no charge because they are Neutral. They are the balancing act in each atom.
   o   The proton and electron are Motion and Matter.

If we translate these energies into human terms and traits, the proton becomes the solvent, the principle of Separation, the individualizing part of the atom. It is the Principle of Radiation at work throughout Life. It is light and all movement. It is the Father.

The electron is the glue that holds it all together. It is the Principle of Fusion at work in life, causing all Matter to manifest, and all connection and relationships to take place. It is the Mother.

The neutron is the Child. It keeps the balance between the electron and proton. It creates our future. Just as the Universe demonstrates for us to see, Life is lived from the center outwards. The neutron, the Creator, sits in the center of each atom. The Proton/Father and the Electron/Mother within each atom constantly interact with each other and their blended energy is sent to the Neutron/Child, who then creates the future with it.

The Theory of Relativity/Einstein's alternate theory of gravity, postulated in 1915, said that the universe is bent and curved out of shape by every moon, star and galaxy in it and all energy has to follow these curves, from the smallest to the largest, including beams of light and motes of dust.

Today, Physics and Cosmology have developed a new scientific Creation story for the atom. This story tells us that everything in the world is made of atoms, and how atoms came to be.
Many scientists now believe that the path to understanding ourselves lies in understanding the birth and death of stars, and that the stories of the universe, the galaxies and stars, are our stories. To understand the life process of a star is to understand our Hue-man history.

Science's Creation story says that the first elements were forged in the galaxy during the Big Bang, almost fourteen billion years ago, and that the catastrophic death of a star brings all kinds of new life to the universe, and that every piece of us was forged in the furnaces of a dying star.

Here's the process:

Stars are born in a stellar nursery called a nebula. Each star burns for eons of time, until their need for fuel causes them to expand until they become red giants and finally explode. In that instant after the explosion, sub atomic particles acquire mass for the first time. Particles of mass called quarks are formed. While the star is cooling, the quarks form more complex structures called protons and neutrons. Those quarks are the core building blocks of the atom, which in turn are the core building blocks of the elements.

All of the other elements can be made from hydrogen, which has one proton and one electron in each atom. Helium is the second simplest element with two protons and two electrons per atom.
This basic building material for everything is put in place in the first few seconds after the dying star explodes.

The star continues to go through a series of heating and cooling events, dying in stages, enabling the organizing of more and different elements into their complexity by adding more and more protons, electrons, and neutrons to each atom.

Hydrogen is the simplest element. All stars burn hydrogen. When they run out of it, they begin to die. The star expands into a huge size that it cannot maintain. Then it explodes.

It starts to cool, a red giant dying in stages. It is in these stages that the elements are formed.

In stage one, it runs out of hydrogen.

In stage two, helium nuclei fuse together, forming carbon and oxygen in the heart of the dying star.

In stage three, carbon fuses with aluminum, magnesium, sodium, and neon.

Everything is made of the same basic ingredients, carbon and calcium.

Elements are rarely formed by themselves. They are combined forms. Elements by themselves are extremely reactive. It is this reactivity that enables the elements to combine with one another to make new substances. That makes for an endless variety on earth, including us.

Each stage is hotter than the last, until becomes almost all iron, and the fusion process stops. During the implosion the first twenty six elements are formed naturally.

There are sixty elements heavier than iron, that occur naturally, that are only forged in rare conditions that last about one minute once every hundred years. In that one minute, all of those sixty natural elements are created. The stars producing these rare conditions have to be at least nine times the size of our sun.

The star has to be that big to be hot enough to create through fusion, the rarer sixty elements such as platinum and gold.

Theses stars are called super novas, and in their final death throes, shoot out the elements. One of the things those elements do is to create a nebula, a birth nursery for stars to be born in. Because a super nova event occurs about once every hundred years, the elements created by them in their final stage of death are found in limited amounts on Earth.

The assembly process for building the elements is called nuclear fusion. That process can only happen in the biggest of stars.

We contain the entire history of the universe. Our beginnings go far past the dawn of humanity, clear back to the beginnings of the universe. We are made of the universe. We were forged in the stars...

The chemistry of earth extends far out into space. The moon is rich in helium, silver, and water.

Mars is rich in iron- the red planet. Venus's atmosphere is filled with sulphur. And so on.

Encoded in the star light that bathes planet earth, are the keys to understanding what the universe is made of, and the understanding of how each chemical element is formed.

Heated elements give off light, and each set of elements gives off its own particular set of colors.
Sodium is yellow. Copper is blue. Potassium is lilac. Each element has its own characteristic color. These colors tell us what the stars are made of. Each star emits and absorbs the same colors.
Scientists found that there are the same ninety two natural elements in the universe as there is on Earth.

Carbon 12 atoms contain 6 protons, 6 electrons, and 6 neutrons. This is what humans are made of. This internal abundance is due to the triple alpha process by which it is created in Stars. Carbon 12 atoms are Star material, and they are the standard scientists use to measure all other atomic structures. Human beings are made of star material and so is everything else.

That means that we, as human beings, are being fed energy from the universe, the galaxies, the stars, the moons and planets and the rest, every minute of our lives. Our processes mirror theirs. We are responsible for our personal cosmic energies, and for how we use and think of them, and how we forge our relationships with them. Male, female, child; we all are truly a part of all that is. We share equally in the immense opportunities and responsibilities our universe offers us for expanding and understanding more of Life.

Early Atomic Spiritual Philosophy

The earliest Spiritual Atomic theory came to us from ancient India. The Upanishads are part of the four Vedas, a collection of philosophical texts that form the basis for the Hindu religions. These texts are the oldest Spiritual Scripture texts of Hinduism, which is thousands of years old.

The Book of the Upanishads is considered to be one of the most influential books ever written. They were first written in Vedic Sanskrit, one of the oldest languages on planet Earth.

6

The Vedas, the four ancient collections of Indian hymns and formulas containing atomic Spiritual energy structures and philosophies, the (Upanishads), were first translated from Sanskrit in 1657. The title given to the earliest translation was "The Greatest Mystery".

The Veda teachings traveled from India into Persia, (the successive states of Iran before 1935 were collectively called Persia), then into France, where "The Greatest Mystery" was translated into French and Latin.

Many famous German philosophers gave the Veda teachings and the Upanishads great recognition beginning in 1819. The Vedic teachings spread throughout Europe. In America, the "Vedic Scriptures" became popular through authors Thoreau and Emerson.

YukTesWar,(1855-1936)a teacher of Paramahansa Yogananda (1893-1952), is one of the Masters who wrote about the Spirituality of Atomic Structure....His book was entitled "The Holy Science".

Reincarnation

Many Eastern religions embrace reincarnation to explain time and spiritual philosophies. The Vedic teachings, the most ancient theories about Spiritual energies and how they operate in humanity, embraces the concept of reincarnation in support of the idea that energy never dies, it just changes form time after time.

Reincarnation teaches that each time we die we come back and continue in the next classroom, bringing with us the essence of the past lessons we have learned, both big and small. The essence of lessons learned add to our Cosmic growth and change processes. We can't be here and not learn at least some of our lessons. We can avoid some of the lessons, but we are still learning all kinds of things just by being on planet Earth while whirling through space.

The theory of reincarnation gives a larger framework that explains the vastness of universal processes and their time frames. It makes sense to many that one lifetime simply isn't enough to complete the soul's progress homeward.

The concept of Reincarnation is enshrined in the Inuit language itself. They speak of themselves as they always have been, and always will be. No part of them is left out of their language, Past, Present, or Future.

Half of the Christians and practicing Catholics in the Western world today share a belief in one of the several views of reincarnation, along with the more than the three billion people who share that belief as part of their religious practice.

Joseph Campbell said, "Heaven is a place created by mass consciousness. But it is not Eternity."

The Atom's Spiritual Structure: The Holy Trinity:

How the tiny electron and its partner the proton came into existence has been traced back to the beginning of the universe by scientists, and thus back to God or the Creator or Nature, whatever name one addresses the Life force by.

The electron and the proton make up the Dual nature of the life force, while the neutron in each atom balances their blending and interactions, thus creating the future. Ever since the Big Bang, maybe before, who knows? we have had Motion and Matter, the two halves of the life force, going places together and doing things throughout the universe.

The Holy Trinity

The word trinity comes from **Early 17th century: from tri-'three' + Latin unus 'one'.** If we were to use math, it would not be, 1+1+1=3. It would be 1x1x1=1. Thus the term: "Tri" meaning three, and "Unity" meaning one, Tri+Unity = Trinity.

In philosophy and religion, the three parts of the atom are represented throughout life as the Holy Trinity. Symbols for these three parts of the life force appear in all esoteric teachings and in all kinds of structural and in every fundamental form.
Symbols are very useful to humans when spoken language is not adequate enough to convey Inspiration and Awe. Humanity has drawn and structured and created symbols for the Holy Trinity since their beginning, and most likely always will, for as long as humans inhabit this planet.

This is because the Holy Trinity symbolizes the three major or higher elements containing the pure essence of Creation, Spirit, the spark of Life that infuses all of life.

In Christianity, those same three higher elements are symbolized by the Father, Son, and Holy Ghost/Spirit. In human beings the three Major Elements manifest throughout life as Father, Mother, and Child.

Here's the breakdown of the Three Higher Elements residing in every atom of our being:

The Principle of Radiation
The Father Principle:

The Proton is the Principle of Radiation. This Principle causes all separation and expression that takes place throughout all of life. Whenever any kind of Separation takes place throughout Creation, from the least to the largest, it does so through the electric, expanding, positive force radiating out from the Proton.

The Proton is filled with the essence of the electric, masculine Force, and it is the Father principle at work throughout all of life, out of which proceeds all forms of separation and all expressions of the Life Force. Life **expresses** itself through the principle of Radiation.

The Proton governs all forms of communication, separation, individuation, and personality development in humanity. The proton, the positive force, helps us to evolve further through personal Individuation throughout all of our energy planes of existence. It is not possible to manifest on this planet without having a primary relationship with our Father, or whoever acted as a Father for us.

This primary relationship patterning provides us with the pre-disposition to use our masculine, expressive, separating energies in a given manner and pattern throughout all of the planes of energy our bodies reside on.

The patterning for the way we Express ourselves in life is provided by our physical Father. The Father energies are the Color energies, and life expresses itself through them. How we separate ourselves from any and all aspects of life and how we individuate, is patterned by our Father. Sometimes a Father turns his relationships over to one of the patriarchal religions dominant today, or to another male oriented group (such as the military) to provide guidance and connection for his family.

The patterns for relating to females (the Elements) are provided through the Father. Most religions in the world today have lost their connection to Nature and the Elements, and in doing so, denigrate the holiness and rights of the female.
Some religions have become fanatical (a state of mind) because of the repeated daily religious interruptions to the natural train of thought and connection of hue-mans, one to another. The interrupted connection energy then goes to forwarding the religious principles instead of to the hue-manity they are a part of.

Religion may be one of the most separating uses of the principle of radiation, the masculine force in the universe, that hue-mans have ever devised.

The Principle of Fusion

The Mother Principle:

The Electron is the Principle of Fusion. This principle governs all forms of connection and experiencing of the Life force. We have to have a Mother to manifest (Matter/the Elements) on to planet Earth with a physical body. Mother/ Matter provide our bodies, Father/Motion Provides its movement.

Our physical Mother patterned us with our personal patterns of connection and how to do that. She programmed us for how to receive life, for how we connect to, and receive/experience Life. The glue, and the patterning for how much, how little, and when to apply that glue, is the Mother pattern we use for forming every relationship we have, personally and with the universe.

The Mother principle resides within each atom of our being and throughout all of the life around us. Within the atom, Mother is the electron. How life works for us is patterned by our physical Mother, or whoever provided the mothering experience for us. Our Mother patterned our energy bodies on the physical, emotional, and soul planes of energy for every form of connection and how it takes place.

Father and Mother programmed our conscious awareness with their programming. They passed it on to us. But our world is a different place than theirs was, and our job is to expand our conscious awareness past living on "psychological automatic" (their programming) and moving forward into the freedom that discovering that we have more choices than they provided us with brings.

All generations have to deal with the giving up of the old patterns to discover the new. Some people are comfortable with traditional thought patterns and stay in them. But since we are here to expand our awareness of life and to learn about how it works for us and everything else, sooner or later change occurs, and their generations will have to go through the process of moving past known, familiar awareness into a new frontier.

All the forms of fusion and connection throughout all of life take place through the electron force of fusion, the mother Principle. All connection of any kind that occur, do so through the magnetic, contracting force of the feminine principle. The Mother force rules all forms of Manifestation, Form, gravity, and Magnetism.

The electron/Mother energies are known as the Elements, as Matter. In hue-mans, these are the female energies. We have to have Matter (mother) to have a body. That body moves because of Motion.(father) The two systems are balanced by the Child. (neutron)

The spiritual teachings of the elements are secret doctrines maintained under the protection of the Mystery schools. The Mystery schools are in existence to protect the Elemental Kingdoms, to keep the secrets of how life works from being misused by those who have not earned the right to understand the Elemental, Holy Mysteries of the electron, the feminine Nature.

The Electro-Magnetic Principle

The Child Principle:

The Neutron is the Child in each atom of our Being. It maintains the balancing act between the Proton/father and Electron/mother energies as they interact. The Electro-magnetic Child in each atom balances the dance going on between the electron and proton energies, so that they do not implode or explode. The Neutron is the Universal balancing act at work in all of life. It is the position of Nirvana, and Enlightenment, and Heavenly innocence. It is Creation waiting to be born.

The Neutron constantly balances and sends forth the energy it receives from the interaction between the proton/Father and the electron/Mother within each atom to create the future.

Change first takes place inwardly. It is through the neutron/Child that inner change manifests in the outer worlds of form and the future is created.

The neutron holds a very powerful position. We have all experienced being children. How we were treated and what happened to us as a Child matters.

How we treat that Child within ourselves after we are grown, is the key to achieving and maintaining our own personal state of Nirvana, of happiness.

The way our parents patterned us by their treatment of us as children, is the way we will treat the Child we carry within after we are adults. If the Child patterning needs healing or correcting, (and it most always does) then many times, it takes a trained helper to sort it out. That work is one of the most important things you will ever do for yourself.

We are talking about the neutron, about our future and the Child who creates it. There is a neutron in every atom of our being. We don't want our future to be bleak, and it doesn't have to be. Whether we are disabled, ill, in the process of living and dying, we can create a good future to go into, just as the universe does.

The neutron, the Child, the astral body, the emotional body, (it's all the same thing) has to be tended to because it will kick our butt if we don't. The mental body tends to think it runs the show, but the child/emotional/astral body has to be tended to before the mental or any of the other bodies can go forward. That's how powerful it is.

The neutron (Child) sits in the middle of the atom. It is not considered to be an active force because it resides in a balanced electro-magnetic state. The neutron directs the energy released from the relationship the proton and electron are having with each other, (Mother and Father) and creation occurs through the (The Child) and the future is born.

The Neutron is the seat of Conscious Awareness in human beings. In the figure eight spiral, the Neutron sits in the middle where the Masculine and Feminine energies meet and cross. It balances the blending of their energies.
It is through the Neutron's Electro-Magnetic balancing act that "Enlightenment" takes place. Any "aha!' in your life takes place through this principle.

The Neutron is the seat of the great Karmic Principle, which has no judgment for or against anything, but simply does its job by constantly putting out what we are creating for us to look at, so we can make choices about what we are manifesting.

The better the relationship and interaction between the Proton/father force and the Electron/mother Force inside and outside of us, the better off we are. It is wise to maintain a good, respectful, aware and balanced relationship between these dual energies that make up our Life Force as much as possible.

Our physical Mother and Father represent these two Natures in our personal lives. The polarity stressors and tensions between them create our personal patterns, genetics, and environment. The better the relationship between our parents, the better our existence is.

The dual patterning of the internal nature residing within us, manifesting itself in the outer realms of form, is emotionally regulated through the endocrine system. The emotions ride the endocrine system, releasing the chemicals as prescribed by our emotional states.

Matter and Motion blend in a beautiful and terrible eternal dance...of Polarity and Duality

Polarity is defined in the dictionary as being the property possessed by certain bodies by which they exert forces in opposite directions, with a positive pole having power to attract, and a negative pole having power to repel. Although "Polarity" causes it to look like the two forces of Father and Mother are separated within us, they are not. They are interacting at all times with each other, with the energies going to the Neutron to be processed. If they didn't do this, we could not be here.

Here are some combinations that represent the Dual nature of the polarity in life on Earth:

- ¬ Proton---Electron
- ¬ Man---Woman
- ¬ his --- her
- ¬ Male---Female
- ¬ God---Goddess
- ¬ Father---Mother
- ¬ Inner---Outer
- ¬ Yang---Yin
- ¬ Colors---Elements
- ¬ Wave---Particle
- ¬ Electricity---Magnetism
- ¬ Light---Dark
- ¬ Motion---Stillness
- ¬ Straight lines---Circles
- ¬ Expression---Experience
- ¬ Evolution---Involution
- ¬ Questions---Answers
- ¬ Knowledge---Wisdom
- ¬ Mental body---Astral body
- ¬ Sun---Moon
- ¬ Upper half---Lower half
- ¬ Rejection---Acceptance
- ¬ Day---Night

You get the idea.

We experience life through the Electron, and express life through the Proton. Every relationship we have is based on the activity of these two forces, and what the Neutron does with the energy.

This Holy Trinity, the two great life forces, and the point of realization, the seat of Nirvana, have been spoken of by all of Earth's greatest spiritual teachers.

The Spirit Principle:

The Ether Element- (the Unseen energies)

Matter cannot exist without the divine content of the Ether Element.

The Ether element is the space, the Spirit Force in each atom. It is the divine spark of life that resides within each atom. It provides the FUEL (the higher vibrations) for all of Creation. It is the energy that provides for the Higher Paths of Life to be made available to humanity.

This constant renewal process is provided through the **Ether Element.** Our world is based on the laws of this Spiritual Element. Nothing could exist without it. The Ether Element is the Higher (highest) vibration in each atom, awaiting and guiding the dispensation of the atoms highest good.

Again, Sandalphon – rules the structure of life forms within this planet. Rules our Evolution of Consciousness and Form upon this Earth, and the people ruled over by "Souls of Fire", the symbolic name for the Consciousness of the Atom....This is under the domain of the Ether Element.

The Energy Planes are separated by their rate of vibration. The faster atoms move, the more space they have between them, therefore the less mass. As atoms lose their mass, they vibrate faster and move higher. As atoms gain mass, they move slower and drop down.

At certain places, there is a division of these vibrations, and what is termed a causal body resides in this area, governing and relaying the (Etheric) God energies to the energy planes above and below it. The causal body is directly connected to the Etheric web surrounding us, and one might say, reports directly to it, relaying all the forms of intuition and their information. This activity is considered to be upper world and semi divine in that its vibration is higher. It's shielding is represented by the four point star.

Fundamental to existence are the dual characteristics of our internal nature, for they regulate our Causal bodies, the God-Goddess/Mother-Father being the First Cause of the Universe in our divinity.

Through Universal Prime energy, the inner self and the manifestation of that self into the outer realms of Form, we are provided with a causal community, a common spiritual base to interact from.

There are different communities of mass consciousness that assist the Earth in its growth, and we have membership in at least one of them. This membership keeps our causal vibrations on track and stabilized with Intention and Purpose.

Each energy plane has sub-divisions and hierarchies and specific laws within it. It has its own reality and Beings that engage with us. The part of us that is an energy match for that plane of energy, resides in that energy field. Why? To stay alive. In most metaphysical studies, there are four basic energy planes (with sub planes) that correspond to each of the four bodies, the physical, the astral, the mental, and the soul bodies.

Each of these bodies infuse and vivify each other through the laws of density. That means that the more space between atoms, the faster and lighter the body, making it possible for the bodies to interpenetrate each other, to weave together. They fit together. And, you can't have one without the others.

That's just one of the reasons why blue becomes pale blue on the soul planes of energy where the energies vibrate faster than the slower bodies (there is more space between atoms making less Matter for the color energies to manifest through). The farther down or slower the energy, the darker the color becomes because of density (more matter). This scientific principle works the same way with our bodies on all of the energy planes of existence.

On each of the energy planes, our bodies carry the opposing polarity in order to keep the proper balance and stressors in place. We must be both. It is the law of Duality.

This law manifests in human beings through being polarized to either male or female in the physical body.
On the astral planes, everyone has the opposite polarity of their physical plane and this reversal occurs on up through the bodies. If you are male in the physical plane, you are polarized to the feminine/experience/magnetic on the (emotional) astral planes, male/express/electric on the mental plane, and feminine/experience/magnetic on the soul planes. If you are female in the physical planes, you are polarized to the masculine/express/electric on the emotional or astral planes, female/experience/magnetic on the mental planes, and male/express/electric on the soul planes of energy.

Males, being feminine (receptive/ negatively-meaning magnetic- polarized) on the astral planes, have a harder time dealing with emotions than females, who are expressive and positive-electric-on the astral planes.

Reversing the roles, men are larger, usually stronger, and expressive on the physical planes of energy while females are generally smaller, not as strong, and receptive on the physical planes of energy.

On the mental planes of energy, men are expressive and electric (restless) and have a harder time taking in information than females, who are receptive and magnetic and can sit still on the mental energy planes.

On the lower soul planes, men are magnetic and women are electric, but because we live in a patriarchal era of time, at this time, this particular polarity is controlled in humanity by the male energies.

The Earth's Polarity Shifts:

We have polarity on Earth because Earth does not move in a perfect circle. The Earth does not revolve in a perfect circle. This causes it to shift polarity halfway through one precession. It precesses, which means its rotation causes an ellipse, (which is a closed curve) like the top or bottom of an eye shape-to take place at the end of each of 13,000 years or so. This is half way through a complete rotation of about 26,000 years. As the corner of the ellipse approaches, the polarity of Earth begins to shift to the opposite polarity, which it will operate out of for the next, approximately, 13,000 years.

The Matriarchal and Patriarchal polarities take turns running the show on Earth. Because Earth is polarized, we have to be polarized also. We can only manifest here through the laws of Polarity. At this time, metaphysicians believe we are living in one of the end times of the latest era of Patriarchal polarity.

Because we are living in an era in which the male energies dominate, (a Patriarchal Era), the Higher energies have been defined and broken down into what we call religions (usually defined through wars of dominance). These religions run much of the show on Earth as to the defining of the higher vibrations of energy residing within the Earth's and all other Natures they encounter.

In the male/sky god religions, the Electron/Mother is given a male gender, the "Son". The Feminine Force in atomic structure, that being the Electron, is not allowed to be named as being a part of God. All three of the Trinity, at least in western religions, are labeled as male.

At this point in our evolution, we may not know much about what atomic structure and its Higher Nature really is, because our perception is skewed by an overly masculine view. The portion of the knowledge we now have about atomic structure and our understanding of it, is limited through the insistence that it only be filtered through a Patriarchal, linear, limiting system of thought.

The ancient mystery schools that existed before A. D. time, may have understood much more about it than we do today. (Pre-Atlantis and Lemuria)

The last matriarchal era has been evidenced to have run from at least 25,000 B.C., and ended about 500 A.D. We have a very small amount of recorded history / her-story passed on to us about how life was lived in the thousands of years that were polarized to the feminine aspects of life, before time began to be structured into the latest patriarchal, linear system.

Ariadne seems to have been the last of the goddess-woman archetypes we have retained any recorded history of from that era. She lived during the final days of the matriarchal era and the beginning of the patriarchal era. Her experiences at the ending of the matriarchal era are a small amount of the information that was saved, as the patriarchal era began the deliberate destruction to eradicate all of the feminine aspects from their former places of power in human life. Everything was destroyed that might threaten the incoming patriarchal male era of time. Information that might give power to women again was destroyed. No one knows how much information from the matriarchal Era went underground to be retained through the Mystery Schools that have been in existence as long as life has been on this planet.

The new, incoming Patriarchal Era began its stages of development. The people of the times did not understand or know about cause and effect, therefore, they were highly emotional and superstitious. They relied on their philosophers to explain the known world to them. When there was no explanation provided by anyone, then the event was assigned to the spirit world.

The people needed a focus for their creative energy. Over the centuries, they turned to physical and spiritual efforts to express their lives.

They built churches, ever higher and bigger. But since the use of numbers was not developed enough, the buildings often fell down or did not turn out as planned.

From 1050 AD through 1350 AD., there was a church for every two hundred people in the population. This was the most important form of self expression that dominated people's lives. Through building the churches, the people developed civic pride, civility, ethics, moral orders, the beginning developments of moderation and balance.

Naming the Atom

The idea that everything that we see, and do not see, the idea that all matter is made up of the same energy, was passed down through public, philosophical deductions beginning with the Greek thinkers. At that time, there was a much smaller amount of people in the known world. There were no Scientists back then, so the Philosophers, who later became Metaphysicians, acted as explainers of much of the known world as well as the unknown world for the people...

Leucippus-propounded his theory of atomism and his student Democritus carried the theory forward

Democritus Of Abdera, about 430 B.C.

Democritus was the most prominent of the Greek thinkers of his day. He put forward his theory of "Atomism" as a philosophy. He theorized that the universe was made up of various imperishable particles so small that they could not be divided any further, therefore, they would have to be the smallest units of whole life that existed.

Furthermore, each of these minute particles could exist by itself, and everything was made up of them. Democritus named these particles "Atomos" from a Greek word meaning indivisible. They could not be divided. The word "Atom" is derived from the root word, "Atomos". His theory affected not only the philosophical community of the day, it challenged the way everyone living in that era viewed God, and it caused a split to take place between the thinkers of the day.

The Scientists and the Philosophers went off in different directions with "Atomism". Each of them took the theories of the day, and began to examine them from different approaches. At this point, the early Scientific community began to develop and separated themselves from the early Philosophical community. The Scientists began to structure the known world and to make laws to define the world of matter and motion, based on what they observed in the physical world.

At the same time, the Philosophers began to structure the unseen, higher realms of energy that involved the Feeling Nature and a Higher Spiritual Order. The Philosophers began the process of devising and structuring theories about the unseen parts of Life, placing those theories into a collective belief system that looked to the "Higher" things in life for explanations.

Because of the two fold challenge Democritus's theory of "Atomos" offered, it was buried under adverse public opinion for a long time. But it did not die, and eventually became incorporated into enough of the later Philosophical and Scientific teachings to survive. As time went on, the slow gathering of physical evidence to support the theory of "Atomos" came to life once again.

The Greek thinkers realized that if the theory of "Atomos" was correct, and if everything was composed of atoms, that everything was made of the same substance, then there were obvious fundamental substances with physical divisions that the world is made up of. They named these fundamental, simple substances, Elements.

Empedocles 490 - 430 B.C.

Empedocles unknowingly defined the Electron in Atomic structure. He assigned four physical divisions to the Elements, and he named them "Roots". (Plato was the first to refer to them as Elements.)

They were:
- Earth
- Water
- Air
- Fire,

All of which the known world or matter was composed of. He listed the four Elements that could be seen in the physical world.
He said,
"To the Elements it came from,
Everything will return.
Our bodies to Earth,
Our blood to water,
Heat to Fire,
Earth to Air."

Empedocles cosmic cycle

Contention between LOVE and STRIFE

Pure domain of LOVE: HARMONY

Presence of life

Pure domain of STRIFE: KAOS

Life not present

Life not present

Contention between STRIFE and LOVE

Presence of life

Figure 1Empedocles Cosmic Cycle

Euclid's Table of Elements was the first written work that broke down the four basic Elements into more divisions.

Zeno of Elea 5th Century

Time and Motion

In the 5th century, B.C., Zeno of Elea had many questions about how time and space worked in the universe. He developed many theories about them. He is still famous today for his story of Achilles and the tortoise, which in today's time, has been renamed "The Tortoise and the Hare."

Aristotle 384-322 B.C.

He was a student of Plato, who was a student of Socrates. Aristotle took the Greek theories Empedocles had propounded about the Elemental substances, and put them into a linear construct that is still in use today.

Aristotle named the unseen Element "the fifth Element, Ether" and assigned all of the unseen and the unknown world to the Ether element. Aristotle also divided Motion into basic divisions, thus unknowingly addressing the different components of the masculine nature.

Epicurus of Samos   341-270 B.C. - Taught "Atomos" theory along with his philosophies, which were about where matter belonged, and how it excluded itself Spiritually from other parts of Matter.

Lucretius - about 96-55 B.C. - Lucretius was a Roman poet who wrote about Nature and its relationship to the theories of Democritus and Epicurus. He wrote about how Nature divided itself up, and the development of relationships through the natural ordering of Matter. One copy of his work survived, and was put into print in the fifteenth century.

These are but a few of the events and people that were part of the establishing of the new foundations of thinking and spirituality for the young Patriarchal era that was just beginning.

In today's time structure, the motion of B.C. time is considered as having moved counter clockwise, just as the earth rotates counterclockwise. There were hundreds of years between the ending of B.C. time, and the beginning of A.D. time, which moves clockwise. During that era, many Master Teachers came to this planet for the purpose of assisting in the bridging work that had to be done so the new era of life could go forward using the new patriarchal system.

- The Egyptians were using meditation practices in 2500 B.C.
- The I Ching, the development of the grid in Chinese medicine developed around 2000 B.C.
- The prophets of the Old Testament lived around 1500 B.C.
- The Hindu Vedas of scientific, religious thought were written about that same time, 1500 B.C.
- The Buddha was born about 624 B.C.
- Jesus of Nazareth was born about 6 - 4 B.C. D.-30-36 A.D.

By the time the Christ was born, the age of "Enlightenment" had begun. It is speculated that the Christ went away for many years and trained in one or more of the Mystery schools. He was said to have been an Elemental Master, and his story may be about the bridging of the old order with the new. It was after his death that time began to be counted forward, and began moving clockwise.
Counter clockwise is considered to be magnetic, while clockwise is considered to be electric.

Religions sprang up and began to define life and God for humanity. Religious groups wanted to keep the power of the new energies under their domain, and led successful efforts to reduce the duality of the atom into two dimensional thinking, good and evil, black and white. Out of this religiously defined, two-dimensional thinking, emerged the Patriarchal belief that only males had souls.

At the time of the assigning of names of the three parts of God by religions throughout the world, females were not named as being a part of God. Instead, the feminine role was assigned to an "evil" male, who was dark, carried the feminine symbol of the trident, and ruled the underworld. The feminine became associated with being evil.

The natural living out of our lives through the relationship positions that polarity creates, such as opposition, mutability, complimentary, and equilibrium, came under the jurisdiction of the Church. The clergy then had the power to prohibit or sanction the different types of relationships human had, by labeling them good or evil/ black or white.

The Healers

Men began taking over the field of medicine when the Patriarchal Era began, and during the Dark Ages following it. The history of medicine today traces its roots as beginning with Hippocrates and Galen.

Galen, born about 130 A.D. in Rome, was the leading physician of his day. From the four elements, Galen developed the theory of the Four Humors. His theory was the foundation for Healers and Medical practitioners until 1025 A.D. when "The Canon of Medicine", written by Turkic ethnic-Avicenna 1037-981, displaced the works of Galen by becoming the next textbook for medical education in the schools of Europe. It was nicknamed the "Medical Bible", and is still in use today.

The personality being considered in what medicine was needed to heal a patient was dropped, and became the foundation for Psychiatry.
Physicians began focusing on the scientific reactions that the physical body had to chemistry instead, and began insisting that all maladies were based on chemical imbalances. Male physicians labored without benefit of women's medical knowledge, when at least 45 generations of humans before them had used women healer's wisdom and methods instead of pills.

The significant omission of women and the medicine they had practiced for centuries was never documented. Over time, only two types of female healers were still allowed.

One was the "Wise Woman", who had to be old, isolated, sexless and mysterious. Then there was the "White Witch", who was allowed to be a bit younger, but only if she was "innocent".

The Wise Woman held the lineage of her centuries old taught uses of "herbs" (active pharmacological substances). She used herbs, potions, (distilled essences) rituals, (cleansing and structuring), and incantations. (affirmations). Both types of female healer's skills and abilities for doctoring included, rather than excluded, the treatment of the soul, the feelings, and the emotional logical content of the patient.

The common person went to them for healing, while the male physicians watched with contempt. They called the common people ignorant, instead of taking the opportunity to learn from the female healers. The only other treatment available was to go to the Priests, who held in their hands the new socially correct Spiritual method of healing. This consisted of prayer, fasting, leeching, and the appropriate applications of Holy water, which did not work for most people and many times, killed them. The male physicians and the priests of the churches eventually took the power away from women to be doctors. Witch hunts killed off many of them, and the rest became afraid to use their skills or to practice medicine openly.

The Study Of "Atoms" Rises Again

Until the fifteenth century, when the printing press became available, books were not available to the common people in most countries. The church and state held the power of reading, writing, and religious thinking entirely in its hands.

In the **1600's A.D., a** revival of the doctrine of "Atomism" began again. The second rise of the theory of atomism came about through the interest and influence of a French philosopher named **Pierre Gassendi,** among others.

The English scientist and chemist, **Robert Boyle, 1627-1691,** influenced by Gassendi, began the study of "Atomism" as a science. He and others began to develop tools to experiment and observe atoms. They believed that atoms could and should be defined in physical, measurable terms.

Modern atomic theory largely began with **John Dalton, 1766-1844,** who first wrote on the subject in 1803. His hypotheses still remain of real value in chemistry, and to a lesser extent in physics.

Atoms became an accepted fact, giving a foundation to work from for both the Scientists and Philosophers, who both became concerned with the defining of the Atom, driving the two schools of thought even farther apart.

The more scientific tools invented for the exploration of the atom, the farther apart the two systems grew, until they both became convinced that they had nothing in common with each other.

Further divisions began among the two systems, the Scientists and the Philosophers. Chemistry broke off into its own field. Today we have specific fields of study, such as botany, biology, and many more.

We are in the process of experiencing and expressing energy all day long, every day. There are no accidents in Creation and only a small percentage of Chance. All of Creation is self organizing. That is how quantum fields are developed. Energy can neither be created nor destroyed. It just changes. If we step up to the plate, we need to know that we are stepping up into a higher energy vibration, and in order to explore it, we have to stay aware of the fact that we are stepping into uncharted territory for the Self.

Healing

All of human psychology is dependent on the way the two energy systems, the male and female, stay balanced within each person.

The acid, or male, and the alkaline, or female balance in the physical system, is called the Ph balance. All of the organs and their movement work with the Ph balance, especially the digestive and elimination tracts.

If an individual has caused harm to the Form, both the Elements/electron/magnetic-Colors/proton/electric need to be applied to heal them. It is always a combination of both energies that sets up stability and balance. Enough of both energies balance out an individual.
If the energy is overbalanced to the masculine side, use the Elements to balance. If the energy is overbalanced to the feminine side, use the Color energies to balance.

Black Holes

Black holes are feminine points in a universe. They suck life from one universe and connect it to another universe. When a planet out there explodes, it is a temporary blow off valve for an imbalance occurring in that particular part of the universe in the masculine.

A person makes a choice from their conscious awareness, then the proton (Father) expresses what we want, puts it out there, and the electron, (Mother) attracts the energy back to us.

There are always more choices than we have been programmed to know we have. We are unaware of most of ourselves and of the Life going about its business all around us.

Our conscious awareness is seated within each Neutron in each atom of our Being. The patterns it operates through are provided by our father and mother, or whoever acted in those capacities for us. But what worked for our parents, doesn't work for us. It is not about like or dislike, or hate or love between parents and children. It is simply scientific. They programmed us with what they had available in the world they lived in.

How Conscious Awareness Works

Our conscious awareness swivels back and forth between the negatives and positives our parents patterned us with. They patterned our conscious awareness for us, just as their parents did for them. You see what they saw. You have their patterning for viewing Life in a particular pattern.

They taught us how to deal with every male-proton and female-electron in our being. But we live in a rapidly changing world. The new ways of separating and connecting to each other and everything else, are challenging the old programming we are used to. We put it out there with the Colors and bring it back with the Elements.

Character development comes from realizing that we do not have the right to impose our will upon another.

- The Colors are the force of illusion.
- The Elements are the force of reality.
- Integrity is gray, a blending of black and white.
- Impact is the way energy connects.

One must connect to desire in order for form to exist. The faster anything moves, the more its internal clock slows down. You can't have an internal clock without mass or time would stand still. No mass can travel at the speed of light.

And so we come full circle. In human terms, we have been talking about the electron/female when we discuss the Elements, and about the proton/male when we discuss the Color energies. The children represent the neutron and the outcome of the blending of the energies of the electron/mother and proton/father. To translate these energies into their hue-man, spiritual, and scientific names is the beginning of understanding Life.

"Everything in future will improve if you are making a spiritual effort now. Wisdom is not assimilated with the eyes, but with the atoms."

-Swami Yuktiswar-

On down by Avalon
Avalon of the heart
On down by Avalon
Gonna make a brand new start

Oh the holy grail
Baby behind the sun
Oh the holy grail
Down by Avalon

Well I came upon
The enchanted vale
Down by the viaducts of my dreams
Down by Camelot, hangs the tale
In the ancient vale

Oh the Avalon sunset
Avalon of the heart
Me and my lady
Goin' down by Avalon

Well I came upon
The enchanted vale
Down by the viaducts of my dreams
Near Camelot hangs the tale
Of the enchanted vale

In the upper room
There the cup does stand
In the upper room
Down by Avalon

Goin' down by Avalon
Oh my Avalon of the heart
Goin' down by Avalon
Gonna make a brand new start

Oh down by Avalon
Oh baby behind the sun
Goin' down by Avalon
Well the journey's just begun

Oh down by Avalon
Sweet Avalon of the heart
 Goin' down by Avalon.

Song
Avalon Of The Heart
Artist
Van Morrison
Album
Enlightenment

vanmorrisonofficial; EMI Music Publishing, BMG Rights
Management, UMPI, SOLAR Music Rights Management, Abramus
Digital, ARESA, and 4 Music Rights Societies

www.ingramcontent.com/pod-product-compliance
Lightning Source LLC
Chambersburg PA
CBHW061920130726
47908CB00017B/2626